Wanda's Words Got Stuck

For the wonderful Lewisham Speech and Language Therapy team – L.R.
For Jenny (JSN) with lots of love x – P.B.

First published 2020 by Nosy Crow Ltd
The Crow's Nest, 14 Baden Place
Crosby Row, London SE1 1YW
www.nosycrow.com

ISBN 978 1 78800 680 4 (HB)
ISBN 978 1 78800 681 1 (PB)

Nosy Crow and associated logos are trademarks
and/or registered trademarks of Nosy Crow Ltd

Text © Lucy Rowland 2020
Illustrations © Paula Bowles 2020

The right of Lucy Rowland to be identified as the author
and Paula Bowles to be identified as the illustrator of this work has been asserted.

A CIP catalogue record for this book is available from the British Library.

Printed in China

Papers used by Nosy Crow are made from wood
grown in sustainable forests.

1 3 5 7 9 8 6 4 2 (HB)
1 3 5 7 9 8 6 4 2 (PB)

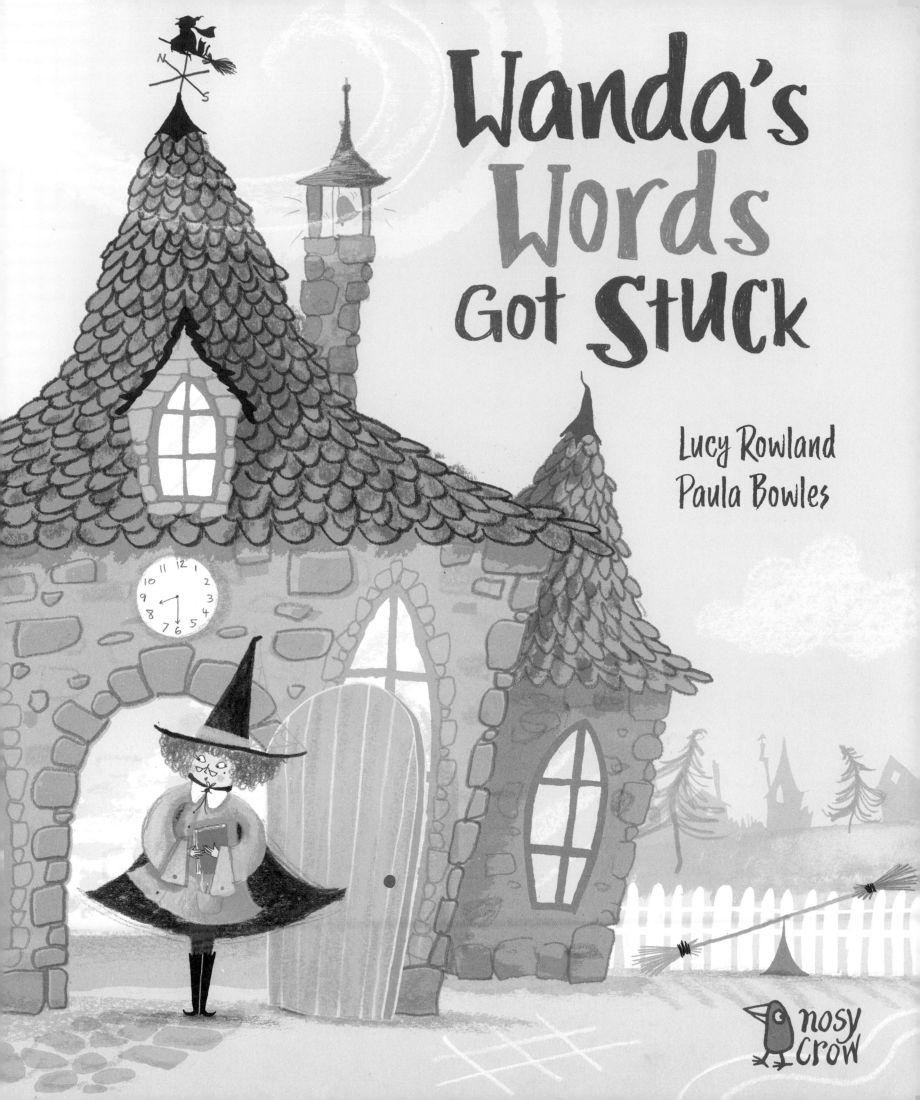

Wanda's Words Got Stuck

Lucy Rowland

Paula Bowles

nosy crow

Wanda the Witch liked tall hats and black cats,
and cauldrons, and potions, and broomsticks, and bats.
She liked to arrive nice and early at school
and read to herself as she sat on her stool.

The classroom was calm with no bustle or din . . .

before the big rush when her class all came in.
See, there was one thing Wanda worried about . . .

... it was talking — she tried
but no words would come out!

It made her feel nervous, so shy and so small.
No, Wanda just didn't like talking at all!

But one day, she thought, "I must try to be brave,
then maybe my words will know how to behave."
So, in registration, she puffed out her chest –
today she'd say, "Here, Miss!" like all of the rest.

First, Isobel answered, then Sam and Jake too,
and Wanda was next, but her words stuck like glue.

Then suddenly . . .

. . . there was a knock at the door,
and in came a girl she had not seen before.

Miss Cobweb said, "This is Flo's very first day.
Let's make her feel welcome. Now, what do we say?"

"HELLO!"

shouted everyone,
all in a rush,

and Flo felt so shy that she started to blush.

Now, some words are meant well
but come out all wrong.
And some are important
(and ever so long).
Some words can be brave,
even if they're just small.
And sometimes, you find,
you don't need words at all.

So, Wanda just quietly waited a while,
then gave a small wave and a very big smile.

She thought, "Maybe Flo's feeling shy just like me."
Flo waved back at Wanda and seemed to agree.

And Wanda and Flo played together that day.
There wasn't too much that they needed to say!

Flo smiled at her friend, and then Wanda just knew
(though she never quite said it) she'd found a friend too.

The next day, in Spells class, Miss Cobweb said, "Right!
The school MAGIC CONTEST is next Friday night!
You'll all need to show us an animal spell."
Poor Wanda went red and she felt quite unwell.

Flo squeezed her hand tight. "We can practise," she said.
But Wanda, uncertain, just nodded her head.

They practised each day after school, in the park,
trying spell after spell as it slowly turned dark.

"Just ONE more!" Flo promised.
"Let's give a big shout!"

Then Wanda watched closely
and waited her turn.
Her tummy felt funny
and started to churn.

Jake lifted his wand, and a black CAT appeared!
And Flo took a breath as the audience cheered.

She conjured a . . .

DOG!

And the dog chased Jake's cat!

Jake magicked a . . .

...LION.

They thought that was that ...

then Flo started chanting a spell,
"HUBBLE BUBBLE ..."
She conjured a ...

...DRAGON!

Oh! He looked
like trouble!

Now breathing out fire,
the dragon swooped low
and turned with a . . .

WHOOSH

towards terrified Flo!

Flo gripped her wand tight, but then — what awful luck —
she couldn't remember her words. She was . . . STUCK!

But then came a FLASH
and a BOOM,
WALLOP, BAM!

As Wanda the witch shouted . . .

And – POOF – then the animals all disappeared!
Flo hugged her best friend as the cloud of smoke cleared.

"Hooray!" the class shouted. Their cheers were so loud that Wanda just beamed and felt ever so proud.

Now, Wanda the witch likes to practise her spells,

and giggle with Flo when they don't go too well,

and chat with her friends during lunch in the hall.
But sometimes . . .

. . . she just doesn't need words at all.